Memoirs of the AntiChrist

John Harris

First Printing: 2015

ISBN 978-1-326-27108-4

www.memoirsoftheantichrist.co.uk

I would like to offer my gratitude, appreciation and admiration to Dan and Ben for all you have done in helping me produce this book. And to someone *so* very special to me, who will always have my heart, who I affectionately call Chic xxx

Content

Prologue

It's funny how many of us truly enjoy a good story, but never take up on the urge to write one ; as they say, everyone has at least one book in them.

Recently I was chatting with my son's schoolteacher and we were discussing what seems to be the dying art of novel writing: Fictitious tales based on what could be deduced as true fact, if the history books are to be relied upon as a source of this.

Recently I was told that I am no author and my writings could be summed up as the scrawling and rambling of a mad man who has most definitely lost his mind, or more aptly, is out of his mind and I suppose to some, this is evidently true. After reading this short story you may come to the same conclusion, but there again you might not, and may actually find yourself seeing past the grammatical issues to see something else that is in all honesty, far more important.

Please appreciate that what I am writing about is done in very small bite-size pieces and I am not being rude when I say this, but for some, their attention span is a little lacking in duration.

The subject matter I am dealing with can at the best of times - even for those of us who are interested in it – be a little monotonous, even though for some reason we still remain interested in it. It is that interest I would like to latch onto with this story. Based on historical events, but described in a slightly different way and from a dissimilar perspective, which, as far as I know, we are still entitled to do. Truth of the matter is, we have never *actually* been entitled to do this, it's just some of us ignore this fact. Is it not, in fact true, that many authors throughout the ages have been penalised, ostracised, imprisoned and even put to death because they dared to have a different perspective that was not the accepted one? All this because they simply dare to have an opinion of their own....

Even more so, this story highlights the power that just one solitary man's words can hold, and what he can achieve, by just simply telling the truth; Revelations that could rock the very foundations of the world we live in to its core, if known.

Hidden for over two thousand years, buried under the sands of time with the hope they would never see the light of day again. With the hope that enough has been done and said to make sure, if this story was ever told, and the revelations it holds are made known to the world, no-one could possibly accept such an occurrence could have ever taken place and that the story which tells of these possible truths, is nothing more than myth.

Chapter 1
In the begining

This story starts a little over two thousand years ago, when a ruling set of tribes (Families) - twelve in all - were having problems with the worship of many Gods, carrying on from the Egyptian dynasties they had descended from. This problem was standing in the way of them being the outright rulers and, more to the point, controllers of all they would and did pervade.

The priest class had lost control and a civil war had ravaged Egypt, and the ruling Families had to flee across the water to a place called Lios for their own safety, occupying the northern part of this land – which, unbeknown to anyone, was their actual home. But the problem of worshiping many Gods had followed them and was already present in their home. Not only was it present, it was even stronger in it's application, and resistance to any other faith or the forced adoption of one.

The problem was that each faith had differences between them, which caused rivalry and division and made the law impossible to enforce, as no common ground could be found. Fast losing patience, the families had to construct something that would outlaw the many gods and bring all worshippers under one umbrella, a kind of interfaith so to speak - in other words - Monotheism.

As hard as they tried they could not enforce this and they knew there were always going to be far less controllers than there were controlled, as always, it was simple common sense.

The main reason they wanted control was to apply taxation

upon everyone, with the only exception being themselves... and on the backbone of this create a Class Division System that would ensure the cogs of the commercial construct they wanted to introduce would always turn, and they would remain at the controls bathed in the earthly luxuries this would afford them, and of course the protection of a hierarchical web to hide behind. This symbolises what some might call Heaven on Earth; for is not heaven truly only where you look down upon others? (Epitomised by the size of buildings that are said to raise to the heavens.)

The main objective was to create a Society within every community: an element that was socially dominant within each community that bound the rest of the community by laws that had to be obeyed - that element being them, the creators of the laws. Social structure was the key to unlock all they longed for. To devise a world based on paying to live and with them being the ones to supply everything that was needed to be purchased to live; including land, food, water and all other basic necessities. This was the concept they were striving to complete and was all that was important to them. A mind-based existence that would in time re-write the very values of life itself, to a point they were non-existent, buried under the weight that was survival paralleled by desire. In truth what they needed was malignant law and a law that had to be seen to be non-human and divine in its application and non-tolerance. Master/slave syndrome devised from a master that was an illusion to be placed in the mind of the believer, the accepter, because it would only work if and only if, the people accepted it. That acceptance was to come from coercion, fear, violence and force; all this delivered by religion, law and education bound by words created by religious/political regimes set up as forms of governance.

A governance that could not be argued with, that would in time turn multiple communities into countries, each with a Society at the helm, all linked back to the original Society.

Threat was the key and all that stood in their way was the

deployment of that threat and how to engineer it on a World-wide scale. How to make sure every Society could be created from a template that existed in a book they would manufacture for that specific purpose, the underwriters if you will, that in time would result in two hundred and ten political regimes spread across one hundred and ninety seven countries, or some would say political prisons.

That was until one man read an ancient text that delivered exactly what they sought, that was completely and entirely un-ethical, corrupt, depraved and perfect, and would rid them of the multi God syndrome, for a while – well until they needed it again. And create what we all live in to this very day, socially engineered control of primitive humans, who went it would seem from worshipping fire to invisible beings in the sky.

And so the story goes....

One ruling family elder had a son named Jesus. Jesus was a bright intelligent diligent student who was particularly brilliant when it came to the matters of politics and was a keen student when it came to history. He studied in particular a pharaoh called Akhenaten and what he was accused of, which in effect, had caused the civil war to rage in Egypt.

Akhenaten was accused of sun worship and accused of bringing into existence Monotheism. (the worship of one God) The people of Egypt rose against him according to historical accounts, because they were still convinced there were multiple Gods, and would and could not accept this new doctrine. This is what the historical records had recoded, but these were not the only records kept from that time, and because Jesus was a member of the ruling families he had access to this other set of records that contained a completely different version of events.

These records proclaimed that Akhenaten had told what he considered was the truth regarding the existence of any Gods; that it was all for control purposes and no Gods actually existed and never had in his opinion. They were nothing but the figment of the imagination of those who desired control, so they could demand a bigger slice of the pie, so to speak. This figment was then placed in the mind of those who needed to be controlled, who would in return supply the labour needed to create all that they would not benefit from themselves, but the controllers (Temples) would. Akhenaten stated that this figment of the mind only worked because the accepter was too primitive to realise that what they believed in could neither be proven or disproven, and that is all it hinged on. Of course they did not realise, as many millions if not billions to this very day still do not realise, that what they believed in was not of their own notion, not their idea, but an idea given to them that quite frankly served but one purpose.

In Akhenaten's opinion some guiding force did actually exist, even though he could not explain what it is or where it is. All he could explain was the fact that he himself had felt its presence in his life many times. He completely understood that because this was known of by those who sat at the top of the hierarchal ladder, but not accepted as being relative, the concept of a God/s could be played upon by explaining this guiding hand's presence within someone's life as being the will of God/ the Gods. This only compounded the illusion in Akhenaten's opinion and only made it easier for the Temple/Families to enforce the construct he called the master/slave syndrome or God complex which created the mental illness called belief – which could result in the believer doing literally anything in the name of that belief if so demanded upon by the Priest Class in the name of a God/Gods.

He also maintained strongly that although yes, you could go against this guiding hand (As the Families and the Priest Class did) and use what is described as free will to commit the most heinous of acts/atrocities, in the end this force/source of simple wisdom would only tolerate so much, until such time as all freely created duplicity would have to be rectified.

For many reasons these records that Jesus was studying intently had to be filed away because of what Akhenaten was expressing, and moreover for what his opinions were regarding what religion calls a Soul. The ancient Egyptian concept of the soul was that it was the human heart. What Akhenaten expressed regarding the human heart was simply what gave it power in his opinion.

He proclaimed that a small ball of energy like the sun was in all our hearts that was fed by the sun itself. And that was the true *us* that powered the bodies we were trapped in and that by being 'sun kissed' (Sunburnt) this somehow enabled this ball of energy to release a warmth emanating from the heart that filled the body with a feeling of absolute bliss. That is why all men, women and children were made at all times to cover all their skin. No bare skin was allowed to be on show to the sun as this was Temu's will according to the Temple supposedly from their illusionary God of all Gods.

This had been in force for many years, as what Akhenaten was expressing had been articulated before by someone very similar to him, and this was known by the controllers.

Akhenaten himself had experienced this anomaly for four days when he to had enjoyed a little too much sun as a young man, but at the time had no understanding of what had actually happened to him. Only later in his life did he start to put the pieces of the puzzle together that led to the most logical and probable conclusion, that in all honesty, was part of what caused him to go against all he was supposed to be, to become all he should have been all along.

Jesus had no interest in this whatsoever, and felt as many regarding Akhenaten's opinions that they were nothing more than the ramblings of a mad-man. A man consumed by notions that were ludicrous...... but he did take note of what Akhenaten had to say next.

Akhenaten had proclaimed that when the Priest Class on behalf of the Families had tried to introduce monotheism, the people themselves rejected the concept and the ruling elite needed someone to blame and who better than himself, being the

Pharaoh – a position that, in all honesty, was only created for that exact purpose, but in reality stood for so much more not realised. Akhenaten proclaimed that they quickly tried to turn the situation to their advantage, but it didn't quite work out the way they had intended, as the people also turned against the aristocracy as well. As their private political army and ancient version of what now would be called the Police, failed in their attempt to protect them because of the numbers involved.

They did no more than to run with their tails between their legs when their hierarchal protection failed so miserably and showed itself for exactly what it was, and in fact *run* is an understatement, considering all they left behind.

Akhenaten expressed that the concept would have worked if it had been applied slowly and within a story environment at its source. To him it seemed that humanity accepted stories far easier than being told it was the truth regarding the subject matter the story was dealing with.

As historic records showed, stories could in fact gain consensus and if employed with the right techniques could in fact turn into unquestionable fact if the believer was bullied enough into believing the story. Malignant stories full of morality coupled with a unseen threat that manifested into a physical threat (at the hands of the creators and benefactors of the story) worked perfectly on the gullible believers.

In short, humanity is far more ready to except a story as being true, than they are being told facts are true, especially if the story offers them a reward for their servitude and obedience... and because of humanities primitive state they would soon adapt and forget, as they considered what they were actually suppressed by to be completely normal.

This in his opinion was the sole reason the Egyptian Book of the Dead was created. Because in fact, the lower class, or serfs as they truly were, were as though dead to the Families, and they held no regard for these *things* and treated them with such disregard as though they were not a living being. They were simply and ultimately an unwanted necessity to the Families, but nonetheless a necessity that was available in abundance and could be disposed of without a second thought.

Although The Book of the Dead dealt with the concept of death, it did act as a way of controlling the 'unwanted necessity' by simply dealing with the right of transit from this earthly plane to the bliss of the Afterlife, coupled with the threat of damnation by being sent to what was called the Underworld, if obedience of the creators of the book was not maintained at all times. Again, this became normal in the mind of the deluded, who would obey unquestionably in apathetic denial that to do this wasn't habitual. But still many who worshipped other Gods and not Temu would not except the doctrine laid out by the book and many sects of individualised religious worship to numerous other Gods sprung up all over Egypt, making it very difficult to bring *all* under one doctrine.

And thus when the introduction of monotheism was first begun by the Priest Class on the bequest of the Families, it failed monumentally, and a civil war raged because the armed guards/soldiers used to try to force this upon everyone were outnumbered some four hundred to one. Plus of course, in-fighting broke out between the individual religious sects as they demonstrated perfectly how religious indifference would prevent unification in one common goal, even if that goal was ultimate peace far from the reaches of the bloodied hands of tyranny that existed perpetually.

Akhenaten had expressed that if the concept of monotheism was to work at all, then all would have to be brought to the doctrine from one simple template laid out in text in one single book using, as he had suggested, the power of stories and enough enforcers to maintain there could be no backlash.

Moreover, the main reason it didn't work was because the concept was flawed from the beginning and even if the concept did take hold, in the end it would be seen as tyrannous and thus self destruct and most probably implode upon itself when the indoctrinated realised that nothing was ever getting *better* and in truth never *had*.

He expressed this process could take thousands of years as the controllers could end and re-create empires (Religious/Political Regimes) as they imploded under the weight of duplicity at will, always taking power by the point of a sword and nothing more. But eventually, in Akhenaten's opinion, the controllers would become far too complacent and push the boundaries way too far and it would be realised that they had taken everyone for fools, and vengeance is a very powerful motive in those who have been made to look foolish.

When this reality of being so fooled finally struck home, and the embarrassment cascaded, the implosion would begin, as all tyrannous processes are subject to failure by their own methods - being used against the tyrants who created the processes as history tells tales of so wonderfully.

Unfortunately it always seemed that the destructors of tyranny through violence became what they were so against, and thus the process revolved like a perfectly oiled wheel on an axle.

In Akhenaten's opinion this would occur time and time again, until such time as all religions and notions of such things as God/s were eradicated from the face of the planet, and buried forever under the sands of time.

Chapter 2
To be relied upon

Jesus found this one conclusion expressed by the rebel Pharaoh to be the most interesting and fascinating. He realised with a little effort a story could be constructed in such a way, that all would in time accept as unquestionable fact, especially in the first instance because the acceptance of the story was demanded through the threat of violence for not accepting it. By recruiting the Roman armies as religious mercenaries the story could be forced down the pallets of the gullible who, would have little choice but to accept or simply lose their lives in the most horrible of ways. And by creating a book of One God, instead of many, the Monotheism could be employed successfully using the book as a basis and template of their laws that must be obeyed, and with other far-reaching reasons that were so obvious.

But Jesus, being somewhat an arrogant fool, chose to ignore the Pharaoh's warning regarding the process of what tyranny results in... to him it was just a numbers game that had to be deployed with precise timing and empirical measures to ensure success.

Akhenaten also refuted the need of any form of Temples (Churches) and any form of worship or obedience to a figment of the mind called God that spewed out into reality, as the Priest Class within the Temples used the temples to disseminate their poisonous manifesto.

Akhenaten proclaimed that many gullible priests within the

Priest Class did actually believe there was a God by the name of Temu and they were its servants, but those who occupied the top slots, so to speak, knew the simple truth.

That their *positions* relied upon the fact that everyone believed in this primitive, man-made concept.

In reality they were the ones, along with the Families that were playing at being Gods, acting out the roles daily that amounted to nothing more than the Temples, those within it, and those who controlled it, being what they proclaimed they served. It was simply based on lies, very simple lies, and he suggested the bigger the lie the easier it was accepted, as the priests who believed in Temu proved without doubt.

Jesus realised that through using Temples (Churches) placed everywhere, increasing in superiority the nearer they became to major cities, and putting ultimate Temples within the cities, that they could be used to maintain the indoctrination, distribute the law, and of course double as places for dishing out punishment for breaking their law.

What would be even more apt was to build these Temples on places of worship used by the old religions, to suggest that God's will was for all to fall at his servants' knees, as God required this, as He was a jealous God. And thus, all must obey the law of one God as demonstrated by the destruction of all the old religions.

Of course, this would add insult to injury, but it would also re-enforce their dominance.

By this time Jesus had read all that he needed to read and was not concerned with anything else.

From what Jesus had read the Families had already put the Temple - the Priest Class - above the Pharaoh and the records had recorded this and the only reason this worked was because they had claimed that they were doing everything in the Pharaohs' name, as the Pharaoh was placed in his position by God (Aka the Families) thus the Pharaoh – unbeknown to him - was also God's (in other words the Families') representative.

Jesus realised quite quickly that this concept worked on the

principle of having one and only one point of reference of law i.e. what was seen as a central point of administration of the law, which was Monarchic.
This handsomely hid the fact that the Monarch (Pharaoh) was not in control of the law by any stretch of the imagination, as that control had been handed to the Priest Class to disseminate on behalf of who really controlled the creation and administration of the law. Thus a point of blame had been created to defer to, if and when that process was needed to be applied.

This as an application was genius, because this built a metaphorical non-penetrative web of protection around the Families to hide their duplicity behind.

This and one other crucial fact had stayed with Jesus; the concept and the word which was Monotheism. And the realisation that the Temple – on the Families behalf - would in fact play at being this God and that God's will was always being done, because it was the will of the Temple and a simple thing called law could enforce this will, all the time hiding the real culprits in the shadows.

Strangely enough, feeling these records were not relevant or of any significance, none of the other family members had ever taken notice of them, blinded by their own arrogance as Jesus was. Jesus was far too complacent to heed the warnings the rebel Pharaoh had forewarned of.

For months Jesus contemplated what he had read and started to see how this could be used as a the ultimate system of control and what's more, it would net the controllers of this system everything, and `the law' (wealth) was the key.

But he had to be sure that he had covered every base, and procrastinated over every little detail night after night to make sure that when he pitched his idea it would be perfect.

His job now was just to convince everyone he had thought of this concept, because at the base of this idea was a simplicity that could be claimed and would pay handsome dividends – as enough is never quite enough… or so it seems and poor Jesus was inflicted with the curse that you could never quite have enough.

A meeting was called between the elder males of the families and their oldest sons and second oldest on Jesus' request and they all met. That day Jesus prepared and was to give a corporate sales pitch like none before, because he could see a system, a simple system based on what he had read.

A system handed to him by a rebel Pharaoh and the explanations Akhenaten had made via a book by the name of the Book of the Living, a book based on the text of a prophecy not known of by the masses, nor were Akhenaten's words - but he kept a very crucial part out deliberately that day, that the rebel Pharaoh had cautioned of.

He stood before the Families and on that eve and what we all live in to this very day was created, a commercial construct run by corporations in the guise of religions and this is what he suggested was the way to create Christianity, the forerunner of religious/political slavery through belief across the known world.

And this is what Jesus suggested.

Chapter 3
Important

We will start a rumour, create a story that states there is but one God and he has a set of rules you have to obey, commandments if you will, that we will command of them. To do this we will make this law and we will enforce it through violence and the threat of; for non obedience of our law. But these laws only apply to them (of lower status) and not to us. We will have our own set of laws for us alone, and to use as an enticement privileges, to get those to do what we need to be done, where blackmail will be the order of the day.

This structure is called Social Corporate Hierarchy based on monotheism and the `all' will maintain the `few' (in other words `us') through a commercial construct they will have no choice but to take part in.

Once we have done this we can create more laws based on taxation, crime and contractual penalties for victimless crime and enforce them with harsh consequences for those who do not accept this, our law.

We will create a book of these laws and list what must be done and adhered to and this is where the story comes in. Because to make this book work, you need a story that is full of morality- but morality with a slight twist, a twist supplied by us, which can be simply done based on parables, and is something that cannot be either proven or disproven.

Through a developed SCH we can create a Pyramidal selling/ control scheme, where the lowest strata of the Social Pyramid maintains the strata above, which in turn follows all the way up through each strata, ultimately maintaining the eye of the Pyramid which is Us, the top strata.

Through this simple employment each strata above its preceding one controls the one below it, thus our control is deployed on every level of the Social Structure through every strata. But to achieve this, the top strata must be seen to occupy that position through Divine Will of a very jealous and vengeful God, who is so vengeful he even allows his own supposed son to be murdered.

To be absolutely honest some of the family elders were a little bemused by this, if not a little confused, but they were still willing to listen to Jesus because of the high regard he was held in – unlike his brother John who was held in no regard by any of them, who sat there listening to something he had read about before.

Jesus continued.

The story shall say I, Jesus, had 12 followers called disciples, and only 12, because those of the `numbers' will recognise the significance of this. The story shall say I will go against your Temples and pronounce you wrong in your doings and the disciples will tell of my words of the same. The story will be full of words and stories that I say that are moral and good, but with a twist, the most powerful twist that will be known to us as the myth of Jesus Christ the King of Kings.

We shall add a character called God into this story and call him the father, not just mine, but everyone's, and you must do as I say and only through me can they reach His house which we will call Heaven, as I am but his only son and only through me can you reach this heavenly place. A place of perfection that you will return to when you leave this earthly plane, but only if you obey all the laws we allocate for you to do so.

This story will demonstrate how much I am against the Temple and through my teachings I will turn everyone against it. Then one of my disciples will turn against me and you will arrest me, try me, convict me and crucify me upon a cross.

From the cross I will be taken to a cave, where in three days' time I will come back to life, and the Temple will fall at my feet because of this, and because of the miracles we will tell them I performed and the people I have healed because I am the Son of God.

They will be told that I have walked on water, turned water into wine, fed 5 thousand and we shall say I was born of a virgin, an immaculate conception and born in a lowly stable.

The Temple will claim I died for mankind's sins and thus we have created a means by which we can do as we please as someone has already paid the price. And a representative of me will head up the corporate body (Temple) we will create from this and he will be, for all concerned, the most powerful and the most holy of men.

The image of me on a cross shall be present in every Temple for those worshipers to fall at their knees to, to ask forgiveness and for help and they will accept my word, and the word of my servants (the Temple) over and above everything and anything and never will they question.

We shall use dead speak (Corp-Oration) to hide our intentions and a language called the language of the shadows (Legalese), because everything we do and say shall have dual meaning - one meaning to them (the Things) and one to us that they shall not know of.

This Corporate Hierarchal Structure will infect everything and we shall receive the profits of this (taxation).

We shall own all land and all those who dwell upon it and they will serve us, they will have no choice, as they fear us and the words we say.

Of course, there are many details to consider and put in place, and when this is done and the story is complete, let this be the template.

Let them understand that this is what they are commanded to do by the son of God, Jesus Christ, through the words of my servants the Temple.

Later we shall tell them that I will return when what we have created starts to turn upon itself, because in time it will because it is based upon a lie.

Then we can move to reassert ourselves through law, because we shall own the *words* and all they can deliver to benefit us. We must own all words and their meanings, and change them at will to suit our needs, and tell them that when I return the Temple, my servants shall be rewarded for their service.

It will be proclaimed, by he who says he is I (as the king of kings) that I have returned to save humanity, and all will fall at my feet and fall to my law, which will be the law they already know and obey. By this happening you will then truly own and rule the world.

The Families had listened and to be honest liked what they had heard, and could see the potential of what Jesus was suggesting, but wanted to know what was in for Jesus - who told them that he just required his name to go down in history as The Messiah and that was payment enough, along with all the riches he could wish for, and a new life in a new land.

All the Family members there agreed except one man who was Jesus' brother - a man by the name of John, who, to say the least, was horrified by what his brother was suggesting should be constructed.

John, although he was a member of the ruling Families, was aghast by what he heard, and fully realised the implications of what Jesus was suggesting, even if no one else did - possibly not even Jesus.

He realised that this system could enslave all of humanity in time, based on a lie and in the end, bring humanity to the precipice of it's own self-destruction.

Now John was a *gentle man* who was forever getting in trouble with the Temple and not only his own family, but the other eleven families as well. Sadly, as he would admit, he wasn't always this way, and in fact it could be said he was possibly worse than his brother stood before him. But time and tragedy had changed him to who he was now, which had allowed him to fully understand the true extent of what his brother was suggesting should be done.

John now struggled daily being a member of the ruling Families. He did not want long hair as he was ordered to wear it, because he preferred short hair - long hair, to be honest just wasn't him. When he was a young man he wanted to be with a servant girl that he loved, and was beaten at times because he would not stop seeing her, and in the end she disappeared from him, breaking his heart.

Many were brought to him of equal, but none were her.

Only days after the meeting John was still reeling from what he had listened to and could not get it out of his mind. It was troubling him deeply as the realisation of what horrors would occur if his brother and the rest of the Families got their way. Things were bad enough without this added worry, and the sadness he felt for his lost brother whom he had so many times tried to reach, only to be beaten down relentlessly.

On awaking this particular morn and without hesitation, he decided to lop his hair short, and set about cutting it. When he had finished, he went outside into the garden and stood looking at his reflection in a pool of still water, and happiness came over him like someone had removed shackles and manacles from his ankles and wrists.

Although he did look a sight, as he had not done the best job on his hair, it mattered not to him, as this symbolised his intention to have no more to do with this his way of life, and he had decided he had to leave for his own sanity.

In a way, John was leaving to protect his family from the shame they would suffer, because of the rage that ran though his veins like a fire that would if he allowed it to, be all consuming and destructive, because he would have to voice his opinion, and most probably publicly.

Donning a robe with a hood, he made his way through the city keeping to the side streets till he came upon one of the houses his friends were working on.

Many used robes with hoods at that time that resembled what

the Priests wore, as it was against the law to stop a Priest in public. The sole reason for this was to allow certain individuals in the Families free movement, without acknowledgment of who they truly were.

This was the preferred way of transit for who would be known now as the Knights Templar, who were the Families' and the Priests' private political police force and assassins.

In this day they were known simply as the Templar and had existed as long as there had been Temples, something John had read a long time ago. Although it could be presumed that what he had read possibly was not true, he found evidence in the way they acted and for whom they acted for, that now provided the reason for the conclusion he had made.

Through a short discussion with two of his friends, he acquired some workman's clothes from one of them who was of a similar build to himself, after leaving the building site and going to his friends hovel.

John found it truly disgusting that his friends had to live the way that they did, when so few had so much and so many had so little. What was even more special to him was the fact that his friends never held it against him for what he was born into, despite that it was his very Family that was responsible for the obscene difference in the way people were forced to exist.

John had tried, on many occasions, to become friends with his brother, and also his cousins and other members of the aristocracy, but always, after only a short while, he could not stand to be with them, because of the way they treated those who they classed as being lower than them.

No matter how hard he tried, he could not adopt their ways and he had tried their form of *normality,* if only to please his Mother, Father and brother. But to John, to act in such a manner was far from normal, to obey such laws that oppressed the very people they also belonged to, but had long forgotten they did.

Because normal to them was a life lived in status, based on equity and not equality, and what saddened John even more was when he saw what was classed as the lowest strata, adopting the ways of their masters...

That they believed to have the burden of so much taxation was normal...

That they believed that self-serving politicians (Priests) actually represented their wishes, when in fact, they did nothing of the sort, and only truly served the wishes of their masters...

But this belief was normal to them, and they would consider anyone who voiced opinion against this Social structure to be actually and completely abnormal, and thus they lived under the rule of the Temple's oppression without complaint, and with the acceptance that this was a normal way to live.

This not only confused John, but also generated so much frustration within him that he quite often considered ending his own life, to release him from this state of limbo as he watched helplessly his fellow human beings live so primitively.

John's real friends were those who truly worked, even though both John and his workmen friends kept this, their friendship, very secret. As with the one he loved and had lost, his true friends were the same; friends he could not be seen with, not for his sake, but for theirs.

After collecting the clothes he required, which his friend gave him willingly, he said his goodbyes and made his way back across the city to his home. Once again, he tried to not allow the stark contrast between the living conditions of the rich and the poor to affect him, as this angered him with an anger he found hard to conceal and sometimes control.

Many times he had been beaten down with words and violence for simply suggesting this was wrong, and many times had he sworn to himself that one day he would see this end.

On returning home he made sure the house was empty and that the servants did not know he was there. After gathering a few things together along with some food and after packing them all into a wrap, John left his home for the last time, and then the city, and started walking south.

For the first time John had a sense of freedom and was free from the curse that was his life, before he had embarked on this journey. Many would wish for what was his life for themselves, and were willing to ignore what John could not, just to be able to live that way. But to John it was a curse and one he was thankful to be rid of.

He had no clue where he was going or what he was going to do, but for now that didn't matter, as for now all he required was the air he was breathing and the sun on his face, and the relief he felt in his heart.

Chapter 4
Change

Some days later John decided that to gain the food he would be in need of and the shelter he would require, he would work on building sites, and learn the trades as he made his way south.. the direction that would take him as far from the Families as he could get, but still on his beloved Lios.

No one came looking for him, well, not at first they didn't, and to be honest, they were all glad to be rid of him and, sad as it was, that also included his own mother, father and brother.

Five years passed and Jesus' plan was working, but the story hadn't quite taken off as well as first expected, and there were those already offering political disagreements that added to the problem.

There were those of significance who'd fallen out of favour voicing opinion, and there were those who would never be in favour doing the same, and these voices had to be silenced. Acceptance had to be complete for the story to work properly, and if that could not be achieved, then the majority would have to be gained through harsh and cruel treatment for having an opinion that was not the accepted one.

This was the start of Political Correctness, even though many did not know this was actually occurring or the true reasons behind its agenda. In other words, many could see that the story seemed rather convenient and a little to good to be true for the those who were to benefit from it and the complete opposite for everyone else.

Those that lived where the story was based called it a lie and said no such occurrence had ever taken place and nor were the places they lived called such names and never had been.

It would seem the names all relate in one way or another to the doctrine they were trying to enforce through the story, based around the Families' original home.

The trouble was the Egyptian concept of multiple gods had spread a long way, in fact, further than anyone had truly imagined – even the Boat People themselves were shocked by the acceptance of their inception.

So over the five year period Jesus and the Families had worked very hard on the story, and had chosen aspects of it very carefully; they knew without doing so it would not be believed.

The story was based where it was because the area was already very volatile through religious differences, and the indifference this brought upon the people who lived there.

Jesus and the Families even created a character called Moses in their book The Bible, based on what Jesus had read regarding what Akhenaten had been responsible for. After the civil war had ravaged Egypt Akhenaten collected up as many of his people as he could, who would listen to him and then he led his people from Egypt and took them back to Lios, his original home.

Jesus just added a twist to this by saying that Moses had parted the Red Sea to add the mystical aspect to re-enforce the story, and even copied the fact that Akhenaten had migrated through this very land.

It was known by the records Jesus had read that Akhenaten had in fact led his people directly through this land, so when all the adverse rejections started, a war was waged against them to hush those that knew and they were massacred, and any historical records of this event that had been made were found and destroyed – until such time it was convenient to use the basis of the story to re-write an additional version i.e. by creating such characters like Moses.

This was to be done many times over the ages as acceptance of any doctrine was better than no acceptance at all, and also a created name from three Egyptian Gods gave the families the ideal foundation to hide behind, hiding their true origins. But for now the objective was to make the story stick and also create means by which it could be protected, create means in words by words, which was fast becoming understood as being the most powerful element known to humanity – one that would never be matched by anything else.

The wars were to rage many times and in fact never end. Massacres seem to be very useful to create hatred through religious acrimony, simply used to get those who would not conform to do so. The Families were told by Jesus that religious belief could bypass human emotions, and could cause the ultimate division, never allowing the masses to rise through segregation. United in individual separation as groups, but through religious acrimony and indifference - only ever being concerned with their own belief – never joining as one group.

A perfect scenario in one sense but a nightmare in another, when trying to enforce a common ground in law, but there was an answer and Jesus had read about how it could be achieved....

Through the creation of words built around the core belief system, built from the story itself, the belief the story had created would be protected by simply never allowing it to be questioned. Words such as desecration, profanity, blasphemy, un-holiness, sacrilege and ex-communication offered the protection afforded by their meanings.

What also could be achieved was to build law on the same principle, again as the belief. Protecting it by never allowing it to be questioned, by separating the law-makers from those who had no choice but to obey the law-makers' laws through a `master syndrome' or – in other words - `the God Complex'.

In effect, what was created was nothing more than pure genius, and still the Family members revelled in what they thought was Jesus' idea, when in fact he had read it all and copied it - a modern day version of copy and paste.

Interestingly enough, even though the story was taking hold in many countries the Egyptian empire had controlled, the one place it was struggling more than anywhere else was the very homeland of the Families, and there was a very good reason for this.

Whilst all this was occurring there was another story being told and spreading of a man who tells of what really is going on, how it came about, by whom and the reason for it. A story of a man, who amongst other things was a carpenter, a tradesman who speaks after his daily work and tells a very interesting story regarding a meeting he was witness to. Not only witness to, but part of, or was supposed to be, but wanted nothing to do with it – but was glad he was there and heard what he heard, because this is a *story* that must be told and remembered.

Even though what he talked of made a lot of sense to a few, there were the many who dismissed what he spoke of as nothing more than uncertain doubtful truth (misinformation) or propaganda. Those being the ones who had accepted a proposition for belief disseminated without any form of verification and were asking the same of John to which, he could offer none, only his assurance that what he told of was in fact true, a truth that would eventually be seen by its own hand and most evidently.

Still many refused to accept what they could see with their own eyes, simply because they liked the perks that were on offer, even though they were to the detriment of nearly all the community as a whole that they belonged to.

What John didn't realise was the fact that the story he was telling - regarding the facts of the meeting in which, his brother, Jesus had explained how to enslave humanity to a *belief* – was being repeated and was causing many to question the authorities and the doctrines spreading with the story of Jesus Christ.

What he also did not realise was that what he said would happen from this was, in fact, happening.

This was causing talk of revolution and rebellion. The law and politics within the Church was now being questioned, as taxation was being increased alarmingly, and the divide between those who were rich and those who were poor was increasing at an disturbing rate. What else was being noticed was that the Church seemed to be getting richer, evidenced by the grandeur of the buildings being built, and even though they had an abundance of food, the normal people, as they called them, were starving.

Many were starting to suggest that the words of the Church as being all-loving, caring and the protectors of humanity for this illusionary thing called God, was nothing more than a façade that hid the real agenda of the Church, as being nothing more than Corporate Company only ever concerned with its own wealth.

Wealth and lands that it was stealing from the very people themselves, in the name of this God. The last thing the Church represented or demonstrated was the love they professed to have for the people, as they watched children starve, consumed by their own greed.

Even the lifestyles of those who were within the Church were now being questioned, as they were certainly on the better side of the divide. Food was being stock-piled by the Church that had been sown, grown and harvested by the very people being denied it, and even though most of the people were starving, with children dying of malnutrition, the Church would not hand any food over, unless of course you were of dignified status. No objection could be raised, as to do so was to go against God's will according to the Church, which demonstrated with perfect clarity the heartlessness of the Corporation known as the Church, made even clearer by the harsh and cruel punishments it would force on anyone who did question this will - which to be honest is still so apparent to this very day, just a little under two thousand years later.

About a year after the story was started and spread, the Families launched the Church by using warrior monks, basically Templar, to take over sacred places all across the land, and turn them into shrines dedicated to the memory of Jesus - even though he was living a very comfortable life in India - and double as court rooms and institutes of law.

This was being done with violence and the imposed acceptance of a new entity to believe in, as the new doctrine to be accepted was being forced upon those caught within a belief structure already.

It was suggested and found by Akhenaten that it was far easier to convert and coerce those who held a form of belief, than it was those who held none - for the later; violence seemed to be the key and it worked very successfully.

Five years down the line and they were already being used very successfully to enforce law through the Priest Class, but not as successfully as they would have liked. It was proving that this enforcement was still being rejected by an ever-increasing amount of the people who knew of John's story, simply because what he spoke of was, in fact, happening in front of their very eyes.

John spoke of not only what had happened, but also what would come from it. Unbeknown to Jesus, John and he shared a common knowledge between them not shared by anyone else and because of this John knew what was going to occur.

Jesus' plan was under attack from all sides and the Families needed to correct this, or more to the point, they needed Jesus to correct this problem, as they were not known of by the masses, only by the select few - and were to demand he did so, or at least demand he find a solution that would work.

John by now was nearly as far south as he could be and had been working for those five years on building sites and had picked up quite a few skills - carpentry being one of them. He also had quite a following because of a story he was telling - a story of what really was happening and how he knew, a story that was gaining more acceptance by every passing day.

The story of John the story teller was spreading through word of mouth, and even though many still did not accept it, many were now prepared to seek this man out to listen for themselves, before making a decision on whether he was right or wrong.

John spoke of none of this during the working day, even

though many of his fellow tradesmen would ask him many a question regarding what he knew. But as the working day drew to a close, he would then sit under the stars in the quiet of the night over a simple meal and then he would talk, and answer the many questions posed to him - questions from not only his fellow workmates, but also from the many who had sought him out.

John also spoke of his life before, as being a member of the aristocracy and what he called the ruling elite. How the life he was forced to lead by his parents and his peers was one that was truly against everything he held dear in his heart. That in truth, it disgusted him and left almost a vile taste in his mouth because, in truth, it was a vile existence that was, without question, morally void. To treat other human beings with such contempt as they did, was not just vile to it's core, but was a depraved indifference to human life created by nothing more than a simple illusion, taking its' power from nothing more than words.

Many times as John spoke of this, the tears would flow as what he spoke of brought back the memories of what he was like before the journey of realisation had presented itself, and he had chosen to set foot upon it long before the meeting he had attended.

But as he wept, he was not alone, as many would join him in their own realisation of the very same, although it presented itself on many different levels, but nonetheless resulting in the same outcome – tears. An outcome that carried no embarrassment with its occurrence now, as it did for many before, including John.

For those who still felt this as their journey begun, the kindness found in friendship relieved them of this burden as they realised, with a little help, it was perfectly ok to feel this way.

Many received much help from John's honest reflections of his own life, and the way he now perceived each and every part of it without the burden associated with the denial of trying to avoid what he once was, and the ever-increasing downward spiral as he tried to live up to the social pressures he was expected to live up to on a daily basis, by his peers, and worse still his own family.

Now, he showed those who listened to him his way of release

and was open in doing so, an openness and a relief it seemed most were desperate for, only needing an example to show them how it was possible to achieve this - an example he didn't even realise he was.

John was causing a stir that could not be tolerated, and it was realised that John's actions could result in a backlash that could in effect cause an all out rebellion; even though at the time the Families had no knowledge regarding who this man was, just that there was one.

A messenger was sent by the Families summoning Jesus back to Lios and he arrived back many weeks later incognito, and met with the rest of the Families, who, to be quite frank, were not best pleased.

After being told what was happening, Jesus and the Families realised that they seriously needed to find this man, for obvious reasons, and two Templar were dispatched to find him. This didn't take long as everyone seemed to know his name and where he was heading and the story he had told along the path of his journey.

Only after a matter of weeks the two Templar came across the man they were searching for and to confirm this, they sat and listened to John for four days, after which they were very shocked to finally discover who this man was.

Shocked at the fact that a member of the ruling elite Families would turn his back on the life he was born into and the luxuries that were afforded to him for being so, and shocked at how he had transformed over the last five years into the man they now sat and listened to.

Both Templar had been members of the elite protection squad and knew all the members of the ruling Families, and even though it took them a while to recognise him because of the transformation John had gone through, they were certain they were not mistaken, as John's voice gave him away, even if his looks masked who he really was.

Unbeknown to the two Templar, what they listened to for those four days was to instigate a change in their actions at a future date that neither of them would have ever expected.

Jesus and the Families had instructed the two Templar that they did not want the man arrested or killed when he was found, so the Templar were instructed to only find out who he was and where he could be found and no more, and to report back with the information to Jesus.

Chapter 5
Meaningless discipline

Some weeks later the two Templar reported back with the information desired by Jesus and the Families and a meeting was called where they were greeted by a very shocked group of men, after relating to them what they had found.

They spoke of how they found John on a building site surrounded by hundreds. This building site was across a bay from a hill surrounded by trees where John would rest his head at the end of the day, where he had a small shelter he had built for himself. Hundreds surrounded him on this hill side and stayed there listening to his words. They were listening as he rested and talked of what he had been witness to and the fact that all Jesus' claims were nothing more than a lie.

John spoke of not only what happened in the meeting, but the fact that life would change forever because of this meeting and what was discussed in it, and the fact Jesus was his brother.

The two Templar also spoke of how John was talking of realisation, and how life could be so different through this, and would nullify all the ruling elites were doing if an example was chosen to end their rule from the people and of the people - and they listened intently.

In that meeting was John's and Jesus' father and as the Templar spoke of all they had found out, all eyes in the room turned to look at him. He spoke and proclaimed that his son had to be stopped, or else all they were trying to achieve would be undone. He was asked by Jesus to how he would react if that meant his brothers death would have to occur to stop him? He answered by simply saying "I have but one son. The man you speak of means nothing to me."

It was decided that Jesus would leave with an escort of Roman Legionnaires and Templar to arrest his own brother, who he had suspected of being the only man who could be doing this, after being told of what was happening by the family elders and the fact his brother had gone missing; to have the knowledge of what had been said in that meeting could only be repeated by someone who had been present in it. Jesus was not shocked by the Templar revelation that it was in fact his own brother John they sought.

Some days later Jesus left with his escort of a thousand Roman Legionnaires and two hundred Knights Templar made up of the elite protection squad – leaving two hundred to protect the Families – and headed south on the long journey the length of the land to where John could be found.

Accompanying them were the two Templar who had been sent to find John, even though this was not to their suiting as they were not rested from the previous journey they had embarked on. Even though they had explained exactly where John could be found, Jesus had demanded they be present and show them personally where he could be located.

It was known that the Templar where the most feared of all fighting forces, but still the arrogance of the ruling families shone through when demanding of them. An arrogance that could have cost them everything if the Templar had so wished, but they were bought for a price and many had passed the point of no return by being given a trough to feed from by the families and subsequently had fed from it.

It was simply all about blackmail and rewards for good service; position, standing, status and monetary gain and nothing more. So the Templar did as they were told, but as with all things, underestimation leads to unsound foundations, and it is never wise to build on unsound foundations, as they would later find out.

Nearly three weeks later Jesus and his entourage of Roman Legionnaires and Templar arrived just outside Marasion and camped behind a hillside found to the west of Pensance that overlooked the hillside John slept upon.

Templar scouts were sent out to assess the situation and to listen to what was being said in drinking houses and anywhere else such as market places. To listen to see if John was being talked about, and to see if what John spoke of was being repeated.

The scouts returned from the local areas and what they reported was not at all good, as it seemed everyone was discussing the lie that was the Jesus Christ story and many were already talking of rebellion against the Church, its' greed and its' unfair malignant laws.

More scouts were sent out and this time it was decided that they would cover a wider radius to see how widespread this seditious problem had become and over how wide an area it spanned.

Anyone who lived within the vicinity of the encampment was arrested and held captive, including anyone who stumbled across the encampment, and with every day that passed, Jesus became more paranoid and more dissatisfied with his living conditions – even though to anyone else at the encampment they were certainly luxurious by comparison.

The days passed and slowly the scouts returned, but the news they returned with was not good at all, and certainly did not please the ever-troubled Jesus.

After all the scouts had returned and reported on their findings, Jesus made a decision, and even though he had fetched twelve hundred men with him who were very heavily armed, he decided that this was nowhere near enough.

Jesus decided not to try and arrest John until he had more Legionnaires to help quell any insurrection that would probably occur if they did try. It was obvious now that his brother had a massive following that stretched, it would seem, the length of the land.

Jesus sent word that he needed as many Legionnaires as could be spared, and told of the reason why he needed them, back to the Families.

As soon as the messenger arrived with Jesus' request, they were dispatched without question, as it was obvious the controlled outnumbered the controllers to such a vast extent, and that if an insurrection did occur, it could quite easily spell the end of everything they were trying to achieve.

After many anxious weeks of waiting the re-enforcements finally arrived and set up camp beside the already existing campground and it was expressed to Jesus that because the size of the encampment, questions would start to be asked - not that they already hadn't started – and it would be wise to move upon John and arrest him as soon as possible. Although Jesus could be very conceited at times – a trait all the Family members suffered from – he was at this time willing to listen to reason, as so much was riding on this and it's outcome.

A meeting was held that afternoon between Jesus, the Templar and the commanders of the Roman Legions. They decided that they would wait until John was asleep in his shelter upon the hillside after working all day before they would attempt his arrest.

With everyone asleep they would have the element of surprise and there would be no chance John could escape.

Early the next morning still under the cloak of darkness a Templar scout was sent out and reported back that all but a few were asleep upon the hillside and the opportune time would be now to move against John. The Templar advised Jesus that they needed to take the two hundred Templar and eight Hundred Roman legionnaires to the hillside to arrest John and the rest of the encampment needed to be sent to the surrounding districts to police it and place it under curfew.

The Templar felt that an armed presence everywhere would create the desired deterrent needed to stop an insurrection occurring, considering the numbers they now had at their disposal.

Jesus agreed and the orders were despatched, which was done very quickly throughout the ranks. It was also suggested that if anyone was to protest about what was happening, without hesitation, they should be cut down where they stood with no mercy being shown to them.

Everyone concerned made ready and they all set off leaving a small contingent behind to protect the encampment and with enough time in hand so they would get to the hillside just before dawn, still cloaked by the darkness.

When they arrived some time later they met with a small amount of resistance, which was easily crushed when it was realised how many were their numbers approaching - this took place at the foot of the hillside.

The contingent then proceeded to make their way up the hillside as dawn was breaking as silently as they could, but the noise of so many feet upon the ground could not be masked.

When they arrived at the top of the hillside at John's shelter, John and many others were already awake, after hearing the commotion at the foot of the hill, and of course the ensuing noise from the contingent approaching.

John realised what was happening as he heard the armour they were wearing, and had told everyone not to offer any form resistance at all, that to only remember what they witnessed this day (saying this without the knowledge of what was about to happen).

A few decided to try and make good their escape and even though many were caught and put to death on the spot, a few did escape down the southerly side of the hillside and into the sea - making their way west across to Chyandor (Long Rock).

Once there, the few who had escaped realised the extent of what was going on, as they could plainly see Roman Legionnaires were present policing the streets, and they mingled into the crowds that were present already asking why they were being told to stay in their homes. Even though many did not do as they were told, they were then being confined to the areas they were in, violently if necessary.

The Roman Legionaries kettled everyone in to the areas with a cordon and many were struck down for trying to escape, which only added to the fear already present within many of the people, as they just didn't understand why such a thing was occurring. Although many had heard of John and more to the point the story he was telling, far more were not aware of this and were very confused.

Never had such a occurrence happened here as the people (Cornish) had always lived in peace under what would be called a Duke. Never had they the need of a King, although the Duke was seen as this representation by some.

They lived and worked the land for free off the sweat of their own brows and their communities thrived as everyone had all they needed to live properly, free of the burden of taxation and the conformity to a Society. Happiness had reigned until that fateful day, from which the whole place was to be locked down and later Catholicised in an attempt to bury the truth of this story.

Chapter 6
Power

John offered no resistance and was soon surrounded by the Templar and Roman Legionnaires and as this happened, two Templar moved forward and secured John by the arms restricting his movements. Cries rang out from many of the men and women present in protest of this, and some moved towards John and his captors, but John motioned to them not to intervene and to quieten their voices, as he could see from the Templars' eyes and body language that they would not hesitate in striking down anyone who would attempt to aid him.

The little over two hundred approximately now on the hillside were outnumbered five to one by Legionnaires and Templars who had come for a fight, and not one of John's companions were armed... the majority were women and children.

John knew from memories of what the Templar were from his past that they would not hesitate in the application of what they had been sent there to do. They served their masters well and would do as instructed, regardless of what that entailed.

John stood alone, held, in the centre of all of this as the entourage parted and allowed a hooded man to approach him - stopping directly in front of him head down. The hooded man lifted his head and lowered his hood and revealed that he was John's brother Jesus.

John, on seeing who was stood before him said aloud.

"Jesus, I have been expecting you brother".

As John said this silent gasps could be heard as all that stood there that had listened to John, realised everything he had said was in fact true and Jesus did not in fact die upon a cross, in some far off land, as he stood before them now.

John could tell many wanted to voice objection and shout "liar" and far more with all their might, but John asked them not to by a simple slow shake of his head.

Jesus moved very close to his brother and said in a hushed voice.

"You have brought this upon yourself brother and what will happen to all on this hillside with you - you have brought this on them too".

John did not reply for at that time there was nothing to say to the heartless self-serving monster that stood before him.

John remembered back to when they were boys, and even as a boy Jesus had been a monster, very soon adopting the Families' ways - bullying and intimidating anyone he felt was lower than him.

John saw this as a sickness, but Jesus and the rest of the Families saw this as strength in their world, that they enjoyed through a basic hierarchal system that they held the top positions of – only wishing to extend their power base through the myth of Jesus Christ, a power base as destructive as the myth itself.

The personas they had accepted, the characters they were playing at being, were a disease of the mind that allowed for immorality to be the order they followed and this had been instilled at a very early age. And even though John had been affected by this at first, he soon realised that this was not the way life was meant to be, seeing all life as being on parity.

Granted, not all human beings are born with equal opportunities, but they are all born equal nonetheless.

This, in truth, did not go down well, and lead to Jesus and his cohorts bullying John because he would not do and say what they would, to anyone they deemed of being lesser than them.

John knew what he had done and why he had done it and realised that Jesus and the Families were trying to create an ordered system of above and below, but never on the same level on a world wide scale. And to him it was only right to forewarn people of the Socialistic Control Mechanism sold on the concept that everyone would receive an equal share of the pie, but in reality some were more *equal* than others. And when the control was applied and the reality of what the Social Structure actually resulted in, it was too late, because the Socially Dominant had already taken their places at the table.

As for the rest, they just had to make do with the scraps thrown to them from the table and be grateful there were any scraps at all. And all this was sold on a concept that this was the will of a God, and it was God that wanted us to have a seat at the table of abundance (Divine Rite) and it is his will, you have to beg for scraps from us.

Then the God concept (Syndrome) would over time infect every aspect of life through Commercialism, as the concept was applied as this Business Model was born into existence. Everyone would strive to be the God on top of their own Pyramidal System, creating the table they would throw scraps from to the lower stratas of their own Pyramid. But the catch was these Pyramids were but tiny versions of the Pyramid they made up and held together. They were its nuts and bolts and to this end they would always pay a percentage, in one way or another, to maintain the Gods at the top of the original Pyramidal Scheme. Thus the perfect Commercial Construct was born that through the Temple (Church) would eventually take Communities to Towns, Towns to Cities and then Cities to Countries (Religious/Political Open Prisons) under the principle Commercial Structure of the original Pyramidal Construct. The goal of the Families was to spread this System across the world, to enforce this Pyramidal Slavery upon all the World's peoples, with them as the benefactors of all revenue that was generated. This is what it truly meant to be a GOD, a sickness of the mind that resulted in Greed, Obsession and Desire that knew no limitations in application to self-satisfy.

But what John realised, as Akhenaten had expressed in his

writings, was that any process built around greed could only eventually result in one outcome. That it would eventually, by very definition consume itself through its own archaic application of perpetual singularity, in simple terms, the needs of greed swallowed by the sea that is belief.

This was what the sickness in his brother's mind had resulted in, as with the rest of the Families, and this sickness had infected every Strata of the Pyramidical System they had enjoyed so much in Egypt.

It could be said that if they had not become avaricious with empirical desires, the system would have probably run pretty much effortlessly for as long as they desired it to. But it would seem that with this mental sickness called belief, in whatever form it has been adopted, produces a symptom called self-importance that takes its roots from the needs of greed and this was the sole reason why Egypt had imploded. That duality had presented its corrective hand and forced the implosion, only for his brother to realise how to create the singularity again, but this time how to make it far-reaching and more effective in its application, and that would prevent those deluded with belief from ever realising the duality of the lives they were being led to live.

In Jesus his brother John had always seen that the position (Status) his brother held was a stop-gap, as Jesus had always wanted to have a higher position life, if not the highest.

This was about limitations. It was quite evident to John that once self-importance was imported into the mind of the human being, this set aside certain limitations and thus the goal was to set aside as many limitations as possible, but not without consequence, as has been highlighted.

His belief in his own self importance that he was quite clearly deluded with, had stripped him of all unpretentiousness and left the monster he was now. And this virus of the mind that had so infected his brother had also flowed through the strata's and infected every level, until a Hierarchal web was created and thus the creators of this Pyramidal System could bathe in the protection it offered them.

In simple terms Delusions of Grandeur, later to become known as the EGO as once again human beings created something else to blame to defer such blame for their heartless actions away from themselves. This was the Social Mask, the Persona, the character they were to act in a play called life, where they controlled the script, the set design, the costumes and of course the story the play was based on.

Within this auditorium of life the actors were lost in role-playing that by-passed any aspect of humility and what it is to be human, passed off as normality to those so deluded and too primitive to see past the fact, it was nothing more than a construct of very basic, but effective beliefs used for Social Engineering of very primitive Human Beings. To primitive to realise that the very thing that enslaved them, if reversed, would be the very thing to free them. Too lost in the primitive state of singularity which was the play they were acting in, to realise through duality that they themselves had locked the door to their own freedom, a freedom they didn't even know existed, as belief denied them of this process (Duality) to be able to come to this simple realisation.

Looking into the eyes of the monster that was his brother Jesus standing before him, John could see all this and John knew what was to be his fate regarding what he had done, and in truth he did not regret anything he had said. Nor would he retract any of it and even though this frightened him as he fully realised that this would result in his death, his resolve was to stand by what he felt was right no matter what the outcome may be, even if it really meant the end of his earthly existence. But the fear that now possessed his mind was screaming self-preservation, trying to convince him to do anything to survive, to agree to what ever his brother would demand of him. It created a quandary of such magnitude within his mind; the need to exist and not succumb to the thoughts of death was something he had never experienced before, and even though his resolve was strong within him, he couldn't honestly say, when that moment arose, whether he would succumb to the demands of his mind, or the simple needs of his heart, only time would tell what was to occur and what would be the outcome.

Jesus smiled at John, and then turning away from his brother, he ordered his arrest, and John was clamped in irons by the Templar. Many of the women and children present, watching what was happening, started to cry as John was roughly treated and the irons were clamped tightly to first his wrists and then to his ankles. They then proceeded to escort John from the hillside as the Templar and Roman Legionnaires were called to arms and surrounded the two Templar that escorted John to prevent any interference from those on the hillside with him.

As he was taken tears started to fall from his eyes – not because of what was happening to him and the pain of the irons upon his body – because he realised what was to become of all those who had stayed with him there on the hillside.

His body slumped in despair as the full extent of the realisation hit him and he pleaded to his brother out loud shouting

"JESUS!"

In a voice that resounded across the hillside.

On hearing this, Jesus turned around and waited for John to be brought before him, and as the two Templar brought John to Jesus, he was thrown to the floor in front of his brother.

John was now on his knees in more pain than he could possibly imagine – not from the physical pain he was suffering, but emotional – as he looked up at Jesus and spoke.

"You require only me brother, for it is only I who has done you a wrong in your eyes. Let everyone else go and please do not harm them, for they have done nothing to you and do not deserve what you intend for them".

Jesus replied scornfully

"But Brother, they are witnesses, and they know the truth because of the words you uttered and they heard. Their reactions said it all when I presented myself to you and I did say, you have brought this upon them – you and you alone".

John's head hung low as he fully succumbed to the despair he was now feeling and the absolute realisation of what was about to occur and the fact that all upon the hillside whether they be men, women or children, were about to be massacred in cold blood - because of what he had said and the fact he had told the *truth*.

Again John called out as desperation took hold of him, calling out in attempt to get his brother to retract the order he had given, an order John knew he had given to the Templar previously as he could see it in their eyes.

"Jesus, dear brother, please reconsider, please stop, please don't do what you are about to do. Surely dealing with me is enough; surely my words will just die in time and be passed off as nothing more than just a story".

Jesus moved forward towards his brother and bent down, as he did he whispered into John's ear.

"But brother, is not the story you suggest based on *fact* - and is it not the case, brother, that this fact will be remembered if all who are witness to it have a chance to repeat it? You are responsible for what is about to happen and you alone, and their blood is on your hands and not mine. All you had to do was live the pleasures that life under Our rule affords you, but you could not do it, could you? Why? Because you hold some form of humanitarian principle that says you see yourself on a par with those who are lower than you. Well, let me tell you brother, not all human beings are equal and 'the many' are born to serve 'the few'. It is survival of the strongest and the most powerful; it is just nature at work. Those on this hillside with you are afflicted with the belief that they are equal, well, they are about to find out that this is most certainly not the case and, as I have said you are responsible for this".

Jesus lifted his head and as he did John stared into his eyes and spoke.

"I know, Brother, that who has just spoken is not you; it is the monster in your mind that lives off the need of all you suggest I should have welcomed and embraced. This is not you speaking,

Brother, as I have seen the real you, and listened to your words of pain so many years ago as you buckled from the discomfort of loss, and turned to me for comfort - is your memory so short-lived you have forgotten such an occurrence and the feelings it delivered? If you go through with what you are about to do, you know deep down that one day you will suffer greatly when the monster runs and hides from the pain that Realisation brings... and when you buckle, who will catch you as you fall so heavily from grace? I know I will meet with the same fate as my friends here on this hillside...

So in reality, Brother, you will have their blood, and my blood and your own upon your hands, and also the blood of all those who have already objected and those who will, as in any tyrannous process the tyrant always falls foul of his own tyranny in the end".

Jesus glared at John in hatred and envy as the jealously rose within him as he listened to his brother's words, words his brother had a far greater mastery of than he, and lashed out and struck his brother across the face, which was greeted by a gasp from the watching crowd.

"Take him away" ordered Jesus, and John was dragged silently away, head down as he waited to hear his brother give the order, and as he did, John waited for the screams to start, as the Templar and the Roman Legionnaires set about the task of killing all upon the hillside in cold blood under direct orders of Jesus his 'lost' brother.

As John and his captive escort left the hillside, the Roman Legionnaires and the Templar set about their attack and the blood-curdling screaming ensued and John wept tears like never before. He couldn't even cover his ears, as he was forced to listen to his friends' demise at the hands of monsters commanded by a monster, murdering innocents under a Precautionary Principle.

Even after some time had passed and they neared the bottom of the hillside, John could still hear screams from the women and children and even the men present being slaughtered, murdered where they stood or laid begging for their lives.

Soon the distance was far enough between them and things were silent and John even ignored the pain from his own feet in chains being dragged, as the sounds of death still rang in his ears, as he was tormented by the thought of how he should have never embarked on this journey in the first place, because of what it had resulted in.

But what he spoke of was the truth, so maybe no one had actually died in vain? He questioned himself as the reality of what was actually happening struck home with a force unparalleled.

'Is this actually happening?' he asked himself in disbelief .. it did all seem like a nightmare until suddenly his bloodied bare feet and the chains between them tangled in some rough sharp gorse and he screamed out in pain and then fell silent as he lost consciousness from the emotional and physical pain he was suffering.

Along the route many were there witnessing what was happening to John, even though a path had been taken deliberately so that major places of inhabitancy were avoided, but not all witnesses could be avoided.

They too were captured, collected and slaughtered in an attempt to eliminate all witnesses to the events that had unfolded. But the attempt in all honesty was futile and would result in a threat having to be issued that would actually work perfectly with the story of Jesus Christ, as someone would be going to a cross.

In the meantime.

The bodies of all those slaughtered upon the hillside where being collected up. The bodies of men, women and innocent children, collected and heaped, bloodied and butchered from the heinous atrocity, the massacre that had just taken place.

The Templar ordered the Roman Legionnaires to collect all body parts as well as the bodies, as all evidence of what had occurred had to be destroyed. And without remorse or any form of realisation of the horrific act they had just performed, they did as they where ordered to do and completed the macabre task.

Then they were ordered to bring much wood from the forests and the construction of large pyres were started, and also the construction of a large cross from an aged oak that had fallen.

Whilst all this was happening…

John was taken to the encampment and thrown, unconscious, into the corner of Jesus' tent and a guard remained with him whilst his brother satisfied his thirst and hunger.

After a while Jesus ordered the Templar guarding John to pick him up, and to throw water at him to bring him round. The Templar did as they were ordered to do looking at each other as they did with a look of disgust. The reason for this was because, the two Templar in the tent with Jesus and John were the two Templar who had originally been sent to find John.

Over the period of time they had been involved, with all that had occurred they were fast coming to the conclusion that what was happening was not right at all, and they were now in a quandary.

They had spoken to each other as they had dragged John to the encampment and in truth what they had discussed would have caused their own demise if it had been overheard. Especially considering that for a good percentage of the journey back to the encampment with John as their captive, they had, where possible, carried John and not dragged him.

It would seem that the two Templar had come to a conclusion of their own regarding what they had listened to John talk about, when they first came across him.

It now was very apparent in them that what he had said, in perpetuity, delivered a profound need to question the morals of their masters. And unbeknown to John, and to each Templar, both of them at their own time had sought solitude to weep their own tears, in respect of what they had done to so many human beings on countless occasions. The horrible acts they had performed and the human life they had destroyed in the name of their masters. All this and much more was now haunting them and had created a self-loathing within both Templar and an absolute loathing of whom they had allowed themselves to be mastered by.

John now on his knees still in irons, being supported by the two Templar, after being brought round from his unconscious state was in a world of confusion until reality struck home. Leaving his confused state John started to recover enough to lift his head to see his brother Jesus gorging his face with food and throwing wine down his throat in pure gluttony.

Looking up from his table of abundance Jesus ordered the two Templar to leave John's side and the pair were reluctant to at first, as they felt John could not support himself, but in the end they relinquished as John turned his head to one of them and nodded slowly.

Jesus ordered that the two Templar leave them alone and to just leave the two Legionnaires at the back of the tent.

At first the two Templar hesitated, until Jesus looked at them and said.

"Well"?

Very unwillingly they did as they were ordered to do and left the tent. As they both looked at each other they could see the contempt they shared for this man called Jesus. They realised, as much as they wanted to save John, the sheer numbers they faced with the nationalistic mind-set they were lost in, made any attempt to save John's life futile.

Both Templar knew the full extent of what was about to happen, both of them were fully aware that John was going to die and both of them made a pact, held an oath that very day that this would not be the end of this matter by a long shot.

They both realised that for the next considerable hours they would have to act as being the perfect Templar and set their feelings aside. Both of them knew that they must not intervene regardless of how strong their emotions became to want to do so. All they must do is bear witness to all that was occurring, and both of them knew it was going to be a very long day.

Sometime later as the two Templar were standing outside the tent quietly and just out of sight, but still within ear-shot, they watched as one of the Legionnaires left the tent and returned sometime later with another Legionnaire carrying a holdall made of leather.

Seeing this only confirmed exactly what they both had presumed was going to happen and the anger arouse in them, as they looked on in disgust, as they together knew exactly what implements were in the holdall and exactly what such implements would be used for. Generally you only ever saw this holdall for one very specific reason and without saying anything, as they just looked at each other, they wondered what sought of monster could have this done to his own flesh and blood, his own brother.

Templar when on duty very rarely said anything to each other, unless of course it was something that needed to be discussed regarding whatever mission they were on, or orders they fulfilling at the time. But for the most of the time they remained silent and just observed.

As with any group of men serving together, forming the bonds and friendships as they did, there were always times of humorous mickey-taking and the bravado it displayed, apart from these times, when they just silently did as ordered, but still communicated their feelings and thoughts regarding any given situation they were in.

For many years the Templar order had passed down it's methods of communication, not known it seems by anyone else:

Techniques that included the ability to read lips, sign language, and others regarding principles of body language, and suggestive tones of the spoken word.

It was also not known that the Templar Order had two very distinctly different approaches and many within the order who were 'time served' had absolutely no idea that this apparent separation existed. That is why not all the Templar knew of these techniques, moreover the ones who were taught them were the ones who would rather talk, than draw a sword to someone.

Although on many occasions they had to do the complete

opposite and did as ordered, the divide was very apparent to them and they had been told that this was for good reason that would come to light at some future time.

The two Templar stood outside Jesus' tent were of this persuasion, and were fully communicating with each other - unbeknown to anyone else who might see them on their duties. What's more, they both now realised that John had had a very profound influence on them, so profound in fact, that the two Templar were now devising a way of never allowing what was happening there to be forgotten.

They had talked of all they had witnessed before this day, and what they had witnessed this very day, and had decided that some things just cannot be tolerated. Although they were, at present helpless to help the man who had caused this so profound change in them, they would make sure that this and such other events were remembered, as so they could never be corrupted.

Chapter 7

Striving for completion

Jesus had finished his meal as the two Roman Legionnaires returned with the leather holdall, and Jesus greeted them obnoxiously by saying

"About time".

The Legionnaire carrying the holdall placed it upon the table and the two of them stood before Jesus awaiting further orders.

Jesus turned to them and said pointing at one of them

"You take your place at the back of the tent as you were and you" pointing at the other Legionnaire, said.

"And you return to your commander and instruct him I must not, under any circumstances be disturbed".

Both Legionnaires did as instructed.

John by this time was getting increasingly anxious and uncomfortable and was trying to shuffle himself into a position of more comfort.

This was noticed by his brother who retorted.

"Well brother, was it worth it, was it all worth the discomfort you are now experiencing, and of course knowing that all those people died because of you?"

John looked up and said nothing, just looking sadly at the man who was his brother. John had nothing to say. He was frightened and heartbroken. Still he could not believe that his own brother Jesus would order the murder of so many innocent human beings. Still he could not believe his own brother could do as he was doing to him now, his own flesh and blood.

John's body shock with nerves and on seeing this Jesus did no more than to open the leather holdall on the table before him, removing a very small but sharp knife that in modern day terms resembled a scalpel.

With scalpel in hand he approached his brother smiling as he did, scrapping the edge of the blade against his own finger, insinuating how sharp it was. Not to the point it cut his own skin, but in reflection of what such an implement could do to human skin.

Jesus knew his brother was frightened and was going to play on this to get John to retract all he had said, and moreover attempt to repair the damage he had caused.

Standing in front of his cowering brother, Jesus looked down at him and said

"Well brother, you know what I need you to do, and surely you fully appreciate what I am prepared to do, to get you to do it.
So let's not waste any time, and just tell me how you are going to resolve this situation and repair the damage you have caused."

John looked up at Jesus and said nervously.
"Brother, oh my poor lost brother, does this not disturb you in any way at all that you are doing this to me, your own flesh and blood?"

Jesus replied

"Brother you stopped meaning that to me the day you set forth on this journey to destroy what is rightfully ours, and in fact if I am absolutely honest, you stopped meaning that to me a long time ago."

John responded

"Brother for what reason do you believe that all you seek to have is rightfully yours"?

Jesus glared at his brother as he responded.

"You know why, you have always known why and once upon a time when in fact I still considered you as being my brother, you were the same and sought the same. What our Family and the rest of the Families deserve is all we seek.

Because Humanity is gullible and stupid, and seeks to be led and controlled, such as the animals do. What we are is a reflection of what nature has created all animals to be. We as a species are not separate from this, we are as much part of this development as any other species of animal is. We do as they do. We form Families (Tribes) and we kill other species to feed our Families, and kill those who would threaten our Families.

Nature has a natural Hierarchy present within it and all we are doing is exploiting that fact, to live life the best way we can, and if we don't do it, then some else will, so better it be us and not someone else.

Better to be the master and not the slave, because regardless there will always be masters and of course those enslaved to them. Can you not remember seeing this in yourself so long ago John, can you not recall this, recall that it is better to be a master than to be mastered?"

John was so frightened watching his brother brandishing the knife before him, but just couldn't say that which he knew would possibly save his life that very day.

Through the fear of death he would still have to try and convince his brother to stop all he was doing and would do, because he loved his brother and wanted to reach out to him and to help him find his way home.

John needed to find a strength within him, to set aside his fears and have the courage to say exactly how he felt, and not what his brother wanted him to say. To do that would mean all that had been so horribly murdered would not have died in vain.

To be honest he would rather die this day than be forced to live in a world controlled by monsters. Living and watching humanity suffer under such oppression by such self obsessed tyrants. Watching the world be enslaved to religious doctrines that would eventually end in wars in the constant struggle for control and absolute control, as the original mono religion fought for control over the rest that it had created for ultimate control purposes. To stamp its outright dominance upon them and to be bathed in the profit that was war.

The rebel Pharaoh had expressed this would be the case, as he reflected on the fact that previous history showed quite clearly that there was nothing new under the sun, and these concepts and methods had been tried and failed many times previously.

That Humanity was stuck in a never ending primitive cycle it could not break free from, because of its need to believe in all things God-like, or spiritual.

That it was stagnated by this mental sickness called belief, to the point whenever it did try to move forward from this point, it simply tripped over its own feet, as it was bound by the conformity of its own actions and doomed to repeat all that had been, and it could not see past *that,* to become all it could be without this restriction.

Akhenaten had expressed all this, regarding religious concepts such as monotheism, that because of Humanity's need to control, it would create many Mono Gods. The principle of One God would not work, so to counter this, a number of Mono Gods would be created, but always coming back to the original Mono concept.

In essence; controlled from one source, but through religious books, full of doctrine that weren't dissimilar in application, just expressing it through different Gods and Deities.

Although the original concept was completely flawed, by using this applied logic based on the psychology of primitive human beings, it fulfilled their need to be individual and different, but at the same time, still part of some group I.e. A Family, Tribe or Religion etc.

For many members, the religion they had chosen became a Family to them, and for many lonely human beings that was the sole attraction. Unfortunately to be part of this, they had to succumb to the indoctrination to be so and thus, were trapped in a loop of dependence. A trait that could be exploited, as Jesus and the Families were doing... a trait that revolved around dependence on an external force, which in time would be added to by the word Spirit. Then the external is combined with an aspect of internal to convince the receptor (Human Being) that by very application of this ethos, they were part of that which they have to obey and thus, escape from accepting this was futile, because it was deemed only natural to believe in such an entity as a God.

Application of this ideology, combined with the notion of a internal human aspect is all that contributed to this perfect form of control, that solely revolved around dependence on a God and of course It's servants. (Church)

This dependence was also transmuted through them to their children, and then to their children, and thus the cycle was never broken, revolving around stagnated principles passed down through every generation.

This by very design maintained the perpetual stagnation that held humanity in this never-ending primitive loop, and cycle of being controlled and nothing more.

Chapter 8
Destiny

After thinking about this and considering what he should say, suddenly he found the words he needed to say to his brother Jesus. He fully realised that there was no way back from this situation, as it was now plainly obvious that he could not change his brother, and nor could his brother change him.

John spoke.

"Brother, as much as I want to please you, I cannot. I cannot say what you wish me to say, because it isn't true and I know, no matter what is to happen to me, I must be true to myself.

Jesus' expression changed dramatically, as anger arose in him and John could see this.

Realising this John spoke again.

"Brother please understand, I can only be who I am meant to be. I must do as I choose to do, as you should, as we always have a choice. And granted, a good percentage of choices we make inevitably are the wrong ones, but it would seem that is what being human is all about. All I say to you is this brother...

You have now gone past the point of no return in the eyes of many, but not in mine. What we once were does not mean we are still that as, in every minute that comes we can make a choice to change and embrace who we are right now.

Please relinquish this insanity that has overwhelmed you.

Please find it in your heart to realise that all you will do from this moment on will destroy you eventually, it will crush you under the weight of realising this is not how we, as a species, are supposed to act. What separates us from the animals is simple morals, and more importantly manners that we all have the choice to use, if we so choose to.

The fact that we do chose not to use them, does not distract from the fact we still have them, and that one principle forms the basis of how we could live in equality, void of man-made concepts of control, revolving around greed.

We can choose to use them and that means we can choose to live differently if we were given the freedom to do so, removed from the conformity that is applied control through belief."

Jesus had remained silent whilst his brother was speaking for good reason. He knew now, there was no use trying to convince John otherwise after all his nonsensical ramblings.

He would have to use tried and tested methods to get his brother to undo all he done, to get him to agree to retract all he had said.

Jesus moved towards his brother and grabbed his shirt and started to cut away at it down the middle, to leave John' exposed skin.

As Jesus was doing this John shock with fear. His breath was short and sharp, and his stomach filled with a vile, sick feeling.

Jesus knew his brother was in fear and was going to use this to his advantage.

Brandishing the knife before his brothers face Jesus spoke his demands of his brother.

"It is now so obvious to me brother that is there no talking to you and to try and do so, is nothing but a waste of my time and breath. So I say this to you brother and take heed of what I am saying. You will do as I say, else I will make you do it through, to be honest with you, any method I need to use.

I will cause you more pain than you ever thought you could suffer and I promise you that you will do as I demand of you."

John looked at Jesus and simply said.

"I have nothing more to say to you Jesus, there is nothing more I can say. You are lost and I promise this of you, you will suffer worse than what I will, because in truth this day, my suffering will end, but yours would only have just started and it will last your lifetime".

On hearing this Jesus erupted into a fit of rage and stuck the knife into his brother's skin by his shoulder blade and cut downwards towards John's chest.

John screamed in pain as the knife entered his skin and then cut him open for some considerable length.

The two Templar outside on guard grimaced as they heard the scream and found it hard to contain themselves.

The two Legionnaires on guard at the back of the tent also winced as they saw the extent of what Jesus had done to John.

Jesus turned away and composed himself as the anger subsided within him and picked up a cloth to wipe the blade of the knife clean. Then he turned to face his brother and said.

"So my brother you have chose your fate and now you confession will be penned and you my brother will sign it and this confession will be posted far and wide to say that you lied.

Lied simply to get fame and later to receive monetary gain for your story telling.

Lied because in fact you want to be seen as the king, to be like the rebel Pharaoh you hold in such high regard.

Lied because you were jealous.

This is what will be said of you, this is what the people will think of you. I will disgrace you.... I will destroy your name here in these times. But then and what is far worse I will then write you into our story book and I will use your name, and call you The Baptist, yes The Baptist, how perfect... because my brother you are about to be baptized in pain and by the sight of your own blood. And what is more brother, no-one will know of what occurred here this day. No-one will know of what you told.

No one will know that your own brother, the Savour of Humanity in their eyes, did such as I do to you.

We shall through the myth of Me rule the world and you, brother, will help with your parables. You will help us control the world, you will help us bathe in the luxury it affords us and there is absolutely nothing you can do about it, nothing!"

Maybe that day Jesus might not have wanted to say all he had said so loudly, as two men, two resolute men heard all, and this only strengthened their resolve.

John was now crying, and bleeding profusely from the wound. But for poor John that was not the end of his suffering.

The camp surgeon was called and came to Jesus' tent to patch John up, as his brother did not want him to die before he signed his confession. And even though Jesus could have signed it himself and then written a suicide note and placed it near John's body, where it would be left to hang by the Templar, he would much rather his brother sign a confession and then pen his own suicide note to explain how he could not live with himself after telling such terrible lies about his Family and his beloved brother.

The surgeon did what he could, but the wound was deep and long and there wasn't much he could do for him.

Jesus asked the surgeon how long his brother would survive such a wound, and was told possibly only a matter of hours.

Jesus knew time was of the essence and called for a recorder to come to the tent.

The recorder came and Jesus explained what document he wanted for him to create and how it should be worded. The recorder left to set about what he had been instructed to do and Jesus returned to face his desperately ill brother.

"Brother you are weak and you know this is to be your fate, you will die this day, so make it easier on yourself and write a suicide note."

Jesus leaned forward and put writing material in front of John.

John still crying and barely able to move through the wound he had received, turned his head away,

This only angered his brother Jesus even more who glared at him and then shouted

"WRITE!"

John did no more than turn his head away, sobbing as he did so.

Jesus lost his temper, and as he did he reached out for a heavy jug of water on the table next to him, lifted it above his head and brought it crashing down upon John's head.

John's body slumped to the floor unconscious. Jesus then turned to one of the Roman Legionnaires and ordered him to check if John was still alive. The Legionnaire did as ordered to do and once he had, said that yes, John was still alive.

Jesus then turned and said to the two guards
"Remain here and do not let anyone come in. Stand in the doorway and do not move until such time as I return. I have things I must attend to."

Chapter 9
The sum of all things

With that, Jesus left the tent and the two Legionnaires did as ordered to do and took their positions in the entrance to the tent.

Some time had passed and Jesus had not returned. The two Templar standing outside decided that they had to do something to save John and took it upon themselves to try, no matter how futile it may be.

Both Templar left their positions and moved towards the entrance to the tent. One of the Templar moved inside only to be presented with the two Legionnaires who prevented him from entering. Looking at them in turn the Templar said quite precisely and abruptly.

"Move!"

Both Legionnaires stood their ground at first until the Templar said in a far more assertive way

"MOVE!"

On hearing this and seeing the look in the Templar's eyes, they both moved aside.

The Templar then told them

"Go outside and join my fellow Templar. Do not attempt to return in here until I say!"

Both Legionnaires did no more than to comply with what they had been commanded to do. They knew it was very unwise indeed to defy a Templar.

When the two Legionnaires were outside the Templar moved quickly to John, and gently brought him round from his unconscious state with some water.

This took some time, but eventually John awoke. Confused and still very dazed, John opened his eyes to see the face of the Templar before him.

When he could muster the strength to speak, and when he was more rational, he did.

"Where is my brother please?" He inquired.

"He left some time ago" The Templar replied.

"You must leave here, my Brother will back soon and if he catches you here he will have you killed." John whispered.

The Templar didn't answer straight away and fetched some water for him. John was too weak to sit up at first, but eventually he did, sitting hunched using the Templar to steady himself, still wincing from his wound.

The Templar spoke

"John we need to get you out of here and far from this place. We can fetch horses and I know of others I can trust, please let us help you?"

John lifted his head and implored

"No, I cannot, but I do ask this of you, if would do but one thing, do only this;

Please remember all that has happened here and why I first embarked on this journey. Please remember why I did this and the story I have told, and tell others so this story is never forgotten. That is all I ask of you."

The Templar could see that John was very weak and helped John to lay down again. With tears in his eyes, he had to accept there was nothing more he could do for John, bar just do what John had beseeched of him.

John started to talk in a very soft voice and asked

"What is your name please?"

The Templar answered

"My name is Sirrah."

John spoke again

"Well Sirrah my friend, I know my brother is going to crucify me and I would ask that you burn the cross I am crucified on, with me upon it.

Make it so all can see it burn, as I am going to tell my brother of a prophecy that talks of a burning cross upon a hill side in a place called Lios, and that one day maybe in thousands of years time a man carrying the symbol of a burning cross naturally upon his body, will write of these events. Write a book that will bring that which my brother has created to its knees, and finally will help humanity eradicate the need for belief."

Sirrah enquired of John

"Is this prophecy you speak of true?"

John, although it was painful to do so, turned his head to look in Sirrah's eyes and said

"Prophecies are not meant to be true, they are meant to be brought to life. Just stories, that act as blueprints for gullible primitive Human Beings to believe in. As my brother has created this, you on my behalf, if it pleases you to do so, could create the cure.

Remember my friend, what my brother has created has a flaw, and that flaw can be used in reverse. All that has to happen is that the intentions of the Eye of the Pyramid must change, by changing who occupies that *position*. All you will ever need is one pure human being. Not pure in deed, but pure in intentions, how you achieve this I will leave to you, but I will remind you, you are a member of the most powerful order ever to exist. Maybe that is clue enough for you to realise how this could be achieved."

With this John laid his head down and became silent.

Sirrah could see that John was dying. With tears falling from his eyes Sirrah slowly stroked John's head and John smiled slightly in acknowledgement.

Sirrah then reassured John

"I will do all you have asked of me, and dedicate my life to finding a way to make this possible. That is my solemn oath to you, an oath I will never break."

John smiled slightly again and Sirrah firstly composed himself and then left John's side and then the tent.

On reaching outside he nodded to his fellow Templar and then turned and just looked and stared in the eyes of each Legionnaire in turn without saying a word.

Both Legionnaires knew the message that was being conveyed and they both then hurried back into the tent, to take up the positions they should have been in all along.

Sirrah then confided in his fellow Templar and explained what had happened, and what had been said between John and himself and the oath he had sworn to uphold.

Many hours later, Jesus returned to the tent with the confession in hand, looking very pleased with himself.

He had been talking to the Templar and the Roman Commanders and it would seem that all the people were secured under Martial Law and Curfews were in place, and with regard to attempted outbreaks of trouble from the people, they had been small and easily contained.

Jesus was feeling very pleased with himself indeed, and thus when he walked into the tent he was smiling, and he gloated at his dying brother

"Oh brother what fortune, your followers are such cowards and have run away to hide, so great are our numbers we now have this situation completely contained, so all I need you to do is just sign this confession. I will pen your suicide note and then this can all end for you."

John didn't stir. He had been asleep since Sirrah had left the tent and was unaware that his brother was even back, or that he was talking to him.

Jesus spoke again

"Brother are you listening to me?"

Again John did not reply, still oblivious to his Brothers presence in the tent.

Jesus was not amused by this and did no more than to take some water from a pail inside the tent in a mug and throw it at his brother.

John, feeling the water hit him, woke with a start and for a second wondered where he was. Then the grim reality of his situation struck home, as did the pain from his wound.

By now his brother Jesus was looming over him demanding he sit up.

It was very obvious now to John he could not comply with his brother's demands, and he just lay there still and silent.

Again this infuriated his brother. Jesus demanded the Legionnaires pick his brother up so he could sign the confession "Pick him up!!"

The two Legionnaires did as they were ordered to do. As they did John cried out in pain and they stopped, only to be shouted at by Jesus, roaring

"I SAID PICK HIM UP!"

This time the Legionnaires ignored John's screams and picked him up, so he was in a sitting position and as they did, John vomited.

Jesus looked on in disgust and told the two Legionnaires to leave the tent, and as they did Jesus took one of their swords and placed it on the table beside him.

John was in a terrible state, and knew he was going to die and was becoming weaker, as the pain he was enduring was becoming intolerable.

Jesus then placed the confession in front of John trying to avoid the vomit that had spewed from John's sickened stomach.

Once he had done this he then stood back and spoke

"All you have to do brother, is sign this confession and it is all over for you."

John in tears again and head down, tried to muster the energy to lift his head and speak, but in his dying state this was more than he could do.

John started to speak, but his voice was too soft for his brother to hear.

Jesus moved forward and insisted his brother speak up

"Speak up now John, are you going to sign this confession?"

John spoke as loud as he could

"Come closer Brother."

Jesus did as requested to do and bent down a little so he could hear John's voice.

John croaked

"I told you brother that what you are about to create will be the death of you, as you will not be able to bear the burden of it when you realise what you have created, or when you realise what you have actually done to your own brother. I assure you Jesus you will one day tell the truth of what has happened here, even though it will bring about your demise.

I am saddened for you Jesus, more saddened than you could possibly imagine, because all you will do and all you will create and all that is created from it will end, when the One Who bears The Mark is here and he writes of this.

Brother I will sign nothing as I have done nothing bar tell the truth."

Jesus was a little taken aback by this as he had thought his brother a coward, and his demeanour changed completely as he suddenly felt very threatened by John's words.

"Bears the mark, what mark?" Jesus asked.

But John would not answer. John knew his brother was a worrier, something he hid from everybody with such bravado and arrogance, and he also knew he was very superstitious. Again another aspect of himself he kept very quiet about, and John knew how to play with his mind and with his dying breath that was exactly what he was going to do.

Jesus became impatient and demanded an answer

"Brother, tell me about this mark."

Still John would not speak.

Jesus by this time was getting considerably more angry and took the sword from the nearby table and started brandishing it near Johns face, so he could see it out of the corner of his eye.

Still John would not speak.

Jesus peeled back the bandage the surgeon had put on John to cover the horrendous cut he had caused and then took the end of the sword and pushed into the wound.

John reared in pain and let out a blood curdling scream as Jesus twisted the tip of sword around in the wound.

John grimaced and almost spat out what would be his last words

"The mark that he will carry will be the mark of the 'burning cross', and he will undo all that will be created from that which you have done.. and how do I know this? Because I read more than you did brother, I read the Prophecy of the Sion, did you not, brother? Did you not read what will be your undoing and how it will come about? You will realise all of this, as I said, my pain ends this very day but yours is only just beginning.

You do know one day they will find out this wasn't your idea, that it was an idea you stole, but you didn't tell the rest, did you brother of what this idea results in?

You will know when your pain begins, when upon that hillside where I slept, a cross will burn, and when he who wears the mark is here, once again a cross will burn on that hillside. Burn to mark the beginning of the end of all you created, and that which has been created from it. It will mark the end and start of the full eradication of the primitive mental illness called belief that you have fooled everyone with."

Jesus was so infuriated he completely lost control. He moved round so he stood sideways to John and raised the sword above his head.

"TELL ME YOU ARE LYING!" He screamed at John.

John stayed silent.

"TELL ME YOU ARE LYING!" He screamed at John again

Still John said nothing.

Out of pure frustration and anger Jesus brought the sword down with force, and embedded it in the back of John's neck. Again and again he struck, over and over until he could strike no more. Wiping his brothers blood from his eyes Jesus looked down to see John's head laying before his body, laying before where he was kneeling, severed.

Jesus stood just looking at what he had done, he had even shocked himself. This was disastrous and he had to think of how he could use this to his best advantage. What he had just done could cause a backlash as John's followers could quite easily revolt against the Temple and the Families. And yes they had control now but…

Jesus' paranoia had set in, but then he had an idea, possibly the best idea he, had ever had and he called for the one of the Legionnaires and met him at the entrance to the tent.

"Guard go fetch the Legion surgeon immediately".

The guard did as he was ordered and returned sometime later with the surgeon and escorted him into the tent.

The surgeon looked at Johns' limp body and his severed head before it and then looked at Jesus.

Jesus spoke.

"Stitch the head back on the best you can." he ordered.

The surgeon looked at Jesus, then back to John's body, then back to Jesus and said.

"I will try, my Lord".

Hours later John's body was taken carefully to the hillside and mounted on the cross and the cross was erected.

At dawn all were taken from the towns and villages and marched to the hillside to see John's body crucified upon the cross and Jesus spoke to them

"Now you have a crucifixion and bear witness to it and know this, whoever of you deny the story of Jesus Christ, then this will happen to you and if you forget, then turn to the Temples (Churches) and you will see this image, so you remember.

Let this image serve as a threat, that if you do not obey us and accept our words as truth, then this will be your fate, or worse."

A guard was set, and on that eve the pyres where lit so all could see the silhouette of John on the cross.

The fires raged for 3 days and no-one attempted to go near the cross to recover John's body.

The guards became slack, bored with standing there. On the

fourth evening the guards were overcome by the two Templar who bore witness to what had happened.

Wood was stacked high at the foot of the cross and it was lit, but before this John's head was removed once again.

Jesus was alerted by a guard that the cross on that hill in Lios was alight and burning well, and could be seen for miles around.

He informed also that the two Templar had gone missing, that they hadn't been seen for days and were the ones who had been sent to find John, and that John's head was also missing.

From that moment when the Legionnaire left Jesus after reporting what had happened, that was last anyone ever saw of Jesus. He left the encampment and just disappeared.

About 55 years later a bedraggled old man, wearing clothes that were dirty and ripped, turned up on the streets of Londinium, a man claiming to be Jesus Christ.

Trying to tell a story of how in fact he was the creator of Christianity, Jesus Christ himself, and that it was created to enslave humanity as it had. That it was based on lies. He was arrested by the authorities and put to death for blasphemy.

In his later years Jesus suffered because of what his brother had told him and the fact that the cross on that hill had burnt, which was lit by Two Templar, who not only had listened to John, but bore witness to what Jesus did to his own brother. On that fateful day an oath was made, and that oath was honoured in every way possible. And the advice John gave to Sirrah that day he followed.

Just over 1312 years later the Knights Templar would be disbanded because of this story, which started on Friday 13th October 1307, because those two Knights told the truth of what they had seen on that hillside in Cornwall and the truth of Christianity.

One side remained loyal to the Roman Catholic Church (The Knights Templar –Papal Bull) and those who knew the truth went to ground as the Templar aka The Order of John of the Mount later to be known as The Knights and Dames of the Order of St John of Jerusalem taking all the Templar wealth with them, their sole objective to never allow the truth of that day and the real truth of Christianity to be forgotten. But not only to serve that purpose, but also to serve John's idea of changing the Eye of the Pyramid and allowing the reversal to begin through a Benign Dictator, that needs but one human being!

The hillside was later named the mount by the Cornish people, where John was mounted on a cross. The Catholic Church changed this to St Michaels Mount in around 500ad after two fishermen claimed St Michael appeared to them as an apparition from upon the Mount, but the Cornish people still just call her the Mount, and many of them I am sure, don't know why they do.

It is possible that at that time the story did surface again, and once again the Families who control the Church (Temple) had to bury the idea and create a new one, which it seems they did.

Many things changed in Cornwall at that time and many towns were Catholicised, having the prefix Saint added to them.

Marasion (Mother of John) was changed to Marazion (Market Jew) Marazion sits opposite Mounts bay and it is across Marazion beach you walk to go to the Mount.

An incredibly pleasant walk if you fancy it and I do suggest a paddle in the sea as well!

It is said that a family of Templars emanating from Cornwall have handed down this story and others like it for centuries, which was to make sure they were never forgotten, because one day it would be needed. Handed down in a way they could never be corrupted. It was told to Templar children of one family, when they were no more than a year old.

The Templar call this process the Science of Memories.

To be continued… x

The story of why John's head was taken by the two Templar, will be covered in my next book The KingMakers which will be available in the next few months!

Epilogue.

What John spoke of in this story in some ways cannot be denied, because what he said would be created is exactly the world we live in now. In truth nothing has ever changed as the rich get richer and the poor get poorer.

We pay for everything we need to live, even commodities that are not really commodities and should be free.

Religion is stagnated, Politics is stagnated and the people are just as primitive now as they have ever been, still with need to believe in such things as Gods, whether they be figments of the imagination or football players, or movie stars, or singers, or royalty, or politicians, or just the mega rich - in honesty the list is endless, as it would seem so is Humanity's stupidity.

Still to this day the religiously insane are still infected by the same mental sickness called belief, as they were two thousand years ago, and perform the most heinous atrocities in the name of this belief.

Still the religious wars rage. Still the innocents die at the hands of these religiously insane primitive Human Beings.

Two thousand years later still poverty exists world-wide, but the Church has Billions... do I need to say any more?

So many will wonder why this book is called the Memoirs of the AntiChrist, and do you know what, I am going to let you work that one out for yourselves. Hint. There is a clue in the book...

I know many of you will find this story alarming, if not obscene and possibly some of you will realise some different aspects from it. All I can say to those of you offended by this story is please remember it is nothing more than a story, as in truth it cannot be denied that what you believe in is based on nothing more than a story too!

And why do I say this? Well, again I am sure it is obvious and you don't need me to point it out for you!

I leave you with the words of Albert Einstein…

"The very definition of stupidity is to do the same thing over and over again, exactly the same way expecting a different outcome…"

The one saying that sums up Humanity and how primitive we really are?

DID3021043
L - #0195 - 090221 - C0 - 234/156/4 - PB - DID3021043